Explore!

MAYAN
CIVILISATION

Izzi Howell

Published in Great Britain in 2018 by Wayland

Copyright © Wayland, 2016

ISBN 978 1 5263 0019 5
10 9 8 7 6 5 4 3 2 1

MIX
Paper from
responsible sources
FSC
www.fsc.org
FSC® C104740

Wayland
An imprint of Hachette Children's Group
Part of Hodder & Stoughton
Carmelite House
50 Victoria Embankment
London EC4Y 0DZ

An Hachette UK Company
www.hachette.co.uk
www.hachettechildrens.co.uk

A catalogue record for this title is available from the
British Library

Printed and bound in China

Produced for Wayland by
White-Thomson Publishing Ltd
www.wtpub.co.uk

Editor: Izzi Howell
Designer: Clare Nicholas
Picture researcher: Izzi Howell
Illustrations: Ted Type

copyright.
please apply

Picture acknowledgements:
The author and publisher would like to thank the
following agencies and people for allowing these
pictures to be reproduced:

Alamy/The Art Archive 22 and 24; Alamy/North Wind
Picture Archives 27 (top); iStock/Lagui cover (bottom
right); iStock/doidam10 6; iStock/Angela Arenal 10 (left);
iStock/janniswerner 21 (bottom); iStock/Angelika Stern
23 (top) and 32; iStock/TonyBaggett 23 (bottom); iStock/
haydukepdx 26; Mary Evans Picture Library 19 (bottom)
and 21 (top); Shutterstock/mj007 cover (top left); Shut-
terstock/f9photos cover (bottom left); Shutterstock/K_
Boonnitrod title page (left) and 7 (bottom); Shutterstock/
Leon Rafael 3, 8 and 11 (bottom left); Shutterstock/
Christian Delbert 5 (top); Shutterstock/Jose Ignacio Soto
5 (bottom); Shutterstock/Matt Gibson 10 (right); Shut-
terstock/Kamira 11 (top); Shutterstock/trekandshoot 11
(bottom right); Shutterstock/photoshooter2015 12; Shut-
terstock/Vadim Petrakov 13 (top) and 15; Shutterstock/
ventdusud 13 (bottom); Shutterstock/Svetlana Bykova
16; Shutterstock/Andrea Skjold Mink 17 (top right);
Shutterstock/Eduardo Rivero 17 (bottom); Shutterstock/
Oscar Espinosa 18 (right); Shutterstock/loca4motion 27
(bottom); Shutterstock/Sidhe 28; Shutterstock/Gerald
Marella 29 (top); Stefan Chabluk 7 (top); Werner Forman
Archive/National Museum of Anthropology, Mexico City
cover (top right), 9 (top) and 20; Werner Forman Archive/
Dallas Museum of Art 14; Wikimedia/ Daderot 4 and 31;
Wikimedia/Walters Art Museum, Gift of John Bourne,
2009 18 (left) and 19 (top); Yale University Art Gallery title
page (left), 9 (bottom), 17 (top left) and 29 (bottom).

Design elements by iStock/Kristisha07, Shutterstock/
Macrovector and Shutterstock/Maria Egupova.

Please note:
The website addresses (URLs) included in this book were
valid at the time of going to press. However, because
of the nature of the Internet, it is possible that some
addresses may have changed, or sites may have changed
or closed down since publication. While the author and
publishers regret any inconvenience this may cause to the
readers, no responsibility for any such changes can be
accepted by either the author or the publishers.

Contents

Who were the Maya?

The Mayan sun god, Kinich-Ahau, was often shown as a man with a large nose and square eyes.

The Maya built an advanced civilisation in the rainforests and along the coasts of Central America. The Mayan civilisation started in around 1700 BCE, but it was at its strongest between CE 250 and 900.

Gods and goddesses

Religion was very important in the Mayan civilisation. Gods and goddesses ruled over different aspects of everyday life, such as the weather and the harvest. Each god had many different forms and could take the shape of a human or an animal. The Maya made sacrifices and took part in rituals to keep their gods happy.

Central American civilisations

The Maya were one of many great civilisations in Central and South America before the Spanish invasion in the 1500s. To the north of the Maya were the Aztecs and Toltec, in modern-day Mexico. These civilisations traded with each other and shared ideas, such as the Mayan calendar system.

This statue at the Mayan city of Chichén Itzá is built in a Toltec style. This shows us that the two civilisations were in contact with each other.

How do we know?

In some parts of Central America, a few people still speak the Mayan language and make traditional crafts but their lifestyle is different to that of the ancient Maya. To learn about the ancient Mayan civilisation, we can study the remains of cities and buildings and read written records in books called codices. Archaeologists have found artefacts such as pottery, jewellery and weapons, which teach us about everyday Mayan life.

The Maya threw valuable artefacts into cenotes (underground lakes) as an offering to the gods. Today, divers find objects in cenotes that teach us more about the Mayan civilisation.

The rise of the Maya

Historians think that the Maya's ancestors reached Central America about 11,000 years ago. For thousands of years, these people lived as hunter-gatherers, moving along the coast and through the rainforests to find food and shelter.

The Preclassic period

Sometime between 5000 and 2000 BCE, the Maya started farming. They cut down areas of the rainforest and learned how to grow crops, such as maize. The Preclassic period began in around 1700 BCE. By this time, the Maya had settled in small villages around their farms. As more food became available, the Mayan population grew.

In the Preclassic period, the Maya burned down some trees in the rainforest and turned the land into fertile farmland.

City-states

By CE 250, some Mayan villages had grown into cities. These cities ruled over their surrounding areas, creating dozens of small city-states, including Tikal, Palenque and Yaxchilán. Each city-state had its own ruler, but shared the same language, religion and culture.

The Mayan territory covered land in modern-day Belize, Guatemala, Mexico, Honduras and El Salvador.

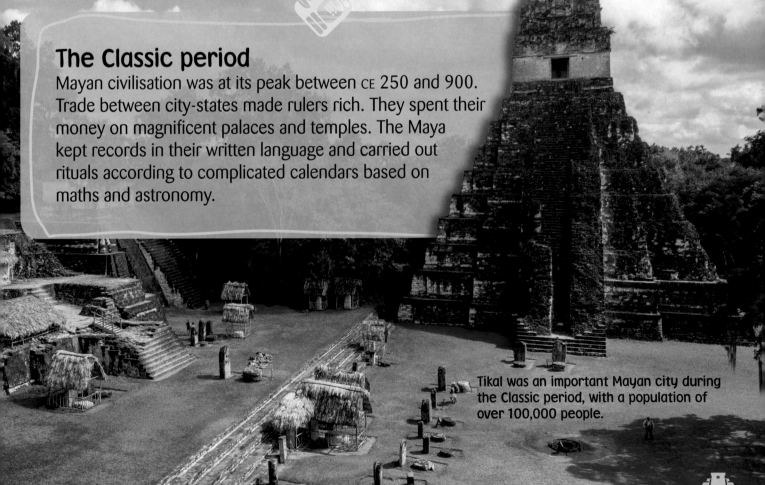

The Classic period

Mayan civilisation was at its peak between CE 250 and 900. Trade between city-states made rulers rich. They spent their money on magnificent palaces and temples. The Maya kept records in their written language and carried out rituals according to complicated calendars based on maths and astronomy.

Tikal was an important Mayan city during the Classic period, with a population of over 100,000 people.

7

Mayan society

During the Classic period, Mayan society was divided between the elite and ordinary people. The elite, which included the royal family and priests, scribes and generals, had most of the power and wealth. Ordinary people worked as farmers or labourers.

Kings and the elite

Each Mayan city-state was ruled by a king, or occasionally a queen. Mayan kings were connected by trade links, royal visits and even marriages between royal families. Kings often went to war against other city-states to secure valuable resources or show their power. Male members of the elite advised the king on these decisions and helped him with tasks such as city planning.

This is a stone bust of Pakal, the ruler of the city of Palenque between CE 615 and 683. Like many Mayan kings, he is shown wearing an elaborate headdress.

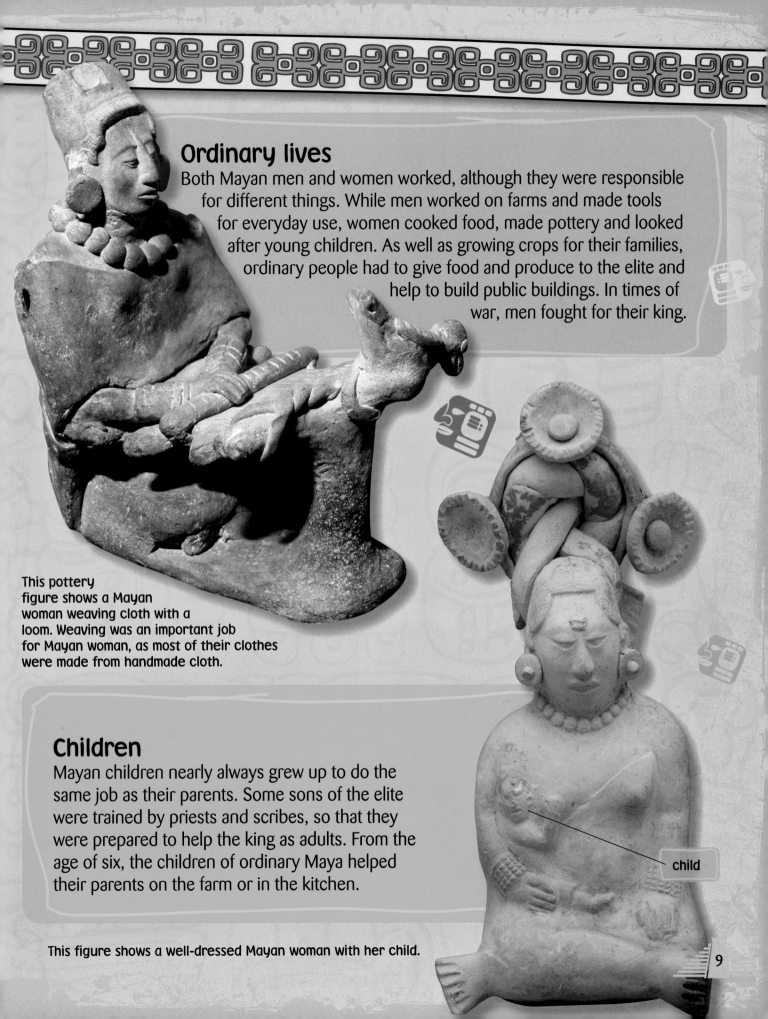

Ordinary lives

Both Mayan men and women worked, although they were responsible for different things. While men worked on farms and made tools for everyday use, women cooked food, made pottery and looked after young children. As well as growing crops for their families, ordinary people had to give food and produce to the elite and help to build public buildings. In times of war, men fought for their king.

This pottery figure shows a Mayan woman weaving cloth with a loom. Weaving was an important job for Mayan woman, as most of their clothes were made from handmade cloth.

Children

Mayan children nearly always grew up to do the same job as their parents. Some sons of the elite were trained by priests and scribes, so that they were prepared to help the king as adults. From the age of six, the children of ordinary Maya helped their parents on the farm or in the kitchen.

child

This figure shows a well-dressed Mayan woman with her child.

The Mayan world

In times of peace, city-states across the Mayan world traded with one another. However, wars between city-states were also common, as kings fought over valuable resources and land.

Trade

The varied Mayan geography meant that different resources were available in each area. These resources were exchanged between city-states across the Mayan world. Coastal city-states had plenty of shells, fish and salt for preserving food. Limestone, jade and obsidian could be found in the mountains. City-states close to the rainforest offered jaguar skins, cacao beans and exotic feathers. The Maya also traded pottery, books and tools.

Two of the most valuable traded items were jaguar skins and quetzal feathers. They were worn by members of the elite as a symbol of wealth and power.

War and peace

Trade helped keep the peace between city-states, as states depended on each other for valuable resources. However, war between city-states was also an important part of Mayan culture. Mayan kings went to war to control trade routes and resources, to show their power and strength and to capture prisoners of war for religious rituals.

In this carving, the Mayan king Bird Jaguar IV of Yaxchilán is shown with a noble prisoner of war from another city-state. The king's posture and large knife shows his power over the prisoner.

Armies

Mayan armies were made up of ordinary men, who were called away from their farms to fight. They were led by kings and elite warriors. As the Maya did not have the technology to make metal, they made their weapons from obsidian, a sharp volcanic glass. In battle, Mayan warriors fought at close range with spears, clubs and daggers.

spear

◀ This mural shows a Mayan army armed with spears.

▶ An obsidian spear head

11

Cities and buildings

Grand stone cities were built in every Mayan city-state. Remains of Mayan cities from the Classic period, such as Tikal and Palenque, can be seen across Central America today.

City centre

Grand plazas, pyramids and palaces were built in the centre of every Mayan city. Giant courts for ritual ball games were found alongside temples, tombs and homes for the elite. Crowds of people from across the city-state filled the city centre to watch religious festivals.

During the Classic period, there were temple-topped pyramids and a royal palace in the city centre of Palenque, Mexico.

City organisation

Mayan cities weren't planned. They grew outwards from the city centre over time, adding more buildings and houses as the population grew bigger. However, they were well designed. Every building was raised off the ground on mud or stone platforms in case of flooding.

Maya built important buildings in the city centre from stone and decorated them with geometric patterns or images of Mayan gods.

Ordinary houses

Ordinary Mayan people lived in small houses on the outskirts of cities or on farms in the countryside. The walls of their homes were made from poles tied closely together and were covered in dried mud. The roofs were thatched with hay and palm leaves. Sometimes, groups of relatives built their houses close together with shared areas for cooking and weaving.

thatched roof

mud

poles

This is a reconstruction of a traditional Mayan house. The houses of most ordinary people did not have any windows, as air passed through the walls to keep them cool.

A day in the life

The remains of ball courts can be see in many Mayan cities. In these courts, the Maya played a ball game as part of a religious ritual. This fictional diary entry describes what it might have been like to take part in the ball game.

The priests wake me and my teammates up early, because today is a lucky day to play ball. We eat maize tortillas for breakfast and I begin to get ready for the game.

First, I paint my body with thick black paint. I protect my stomach, knees and elbows with cotton padding, as the game can be rough. Finally, I place my feathered headdress on my head.

This painted pot is decorated with an image of a ballplayer wearing black body paint and cotton padding.

The priests lead us through the city centre to the ball court. I can see the stone rings on either side of the court and the heavy rubber ball in the centre. My teammates and I need to put the ball through the rings without using our hands to win the game.

As the game begins, I use my elbow to hit the ball to my teammate. I'm glad I'm wearing padding, as the ball weighs a lot. Suddenly, my teammate kicks the ball up in the air and it soars through our ring. One point to us!

After a very close match, my team wins! Even though we are tired and covered in bruises from the ball, I know that our victory has made the gods happy. Hopefully, if the gods are happy, they will give us a good harvest and victory in our next battle.

The diary entry on these pages has been written for this book. Can you create your own diary entry for another person that lived in a Mayan city? It could be a member of the elite or an ordinary person. Use the facts in this book and in other sources to help you write about a day in their life.

glyphs

The stone rings in this Mayan ball court are decorated with glyphs (symbols from the written Mayan language).

Farming and food

The Mayan territory was rich in wild food and animals to hunt, but the soil was very bad for farming. Over time, the Maya learned how to make the most of the land and grow crops.

Farming techniques

The Maya used clever methods that helped them to grow crops in wet swampy areas. First, they dug ditches to drain water from the soil. Then they made raised fields surrounded by low stone walls to keep the soil in place. After a few years of growing crops, they left their fields empty until they were fertile again.

In Central America, maize is still grown in wet rainforest soils. Today, many farmers use chemicals to keep the soil fertile instead of traditional Mayan farming techniques.

Crops

Mayan farmers grew maize, beans, and squash together in the same fields. The squash grew close to the ground, which stopped weeds growing in the fields. The maize grew straight up with a thick strong stem, which the thin bean plants climbed around.

Tamales

This Mayan woman is preparing tamales – steamed mashed maize wrapped in a maize leaf. Tamales are still eaten across Central America today.

Wild food

Mayan men used bows and arrows and spears to hunt animals such as deer, birds and tapirs. They caught fish and shellfish in rivers and along the coast. The rainforests were home to wild foods such as papayas, avocadoes and cacao beans. The Maya made a special chocolate drink from cacao beans that only important warriors and members of the elite could drink.

The Maya hunted peccaries, a type of small rainforest pig.

Art and writing

Artefacts found by archaeologists show us that the Maya were talented craftspeople. They made beautiful pottery, sculptures and jewellery. Many of their works of art were decorated with the written Mayan language, which used symbols (glyphs) instead of letters.

Carving

Skilled Mayan carvers used stone tools to carve images of famous rulers and gods into buildings and large stones, called stelae. The Maya also made intricately carved jewellery and masks from jade, a precious stone. Jade was so valuable that it was only worn by kings and members of the elite.

▶ This jade pendant is carved to show a member of the elite wearing a traditional headdress and large earrings.

▲ This stela shows Uaxaclajuun Ub'aah K'awiil, the ruler of the city of Copán between CE 695 and 738. During his reign, he commissioned many elaborate stelae.

This Mayan bowl is decorated with glyphs (along the top) and a painting of a person.

Pottery

Ordinary Mayan women made simple pottery for cooking and storage, but skilled craftspeople made complex pots and figures for the elite. These pieces of pottery were painted with red, brown and black paints and varnished with a shiny glaze. Rulers often gave each other painted pottery as a gift to secure friendship between city-states.

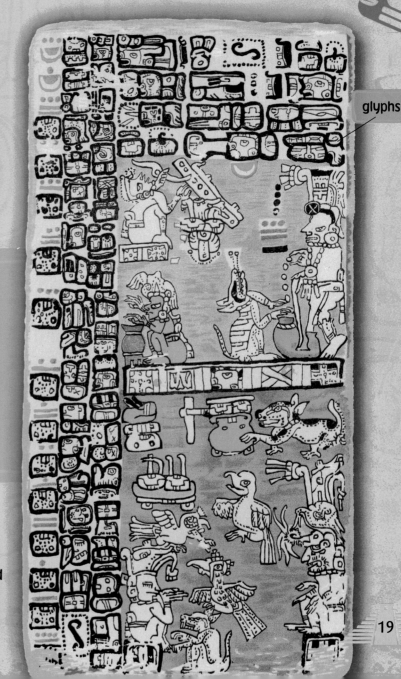

glyphs

Writing

The Maya developed a complete written language, using glyphs to represent both sounds and whole words. The Maya kept records and wrote down stories in beautiful books made from bark, known as codices.

This is a page from one of the three Mayan codices that exist today. It shows information about different religious rituals that happened throughout the year. Some Mayan codices were destroyed by the hot wet climate and many were burnt by the Spanish in the 16th century.

Calendars
and astronomy

The glyphs in this stone carving represent the date 11 February CE 526 in our calendar.

The Maya were talented mathematicians and astronomers. They used their skills to create several complex calendars, which were used across Central America.

Calendars
The two main Mayan calendars were the 260-day religious Tzolk'in calendar and the 365-day Haab calendar. The Haab calendar followed the orbit of the Sun in the same way as our modern calendar. It was divided into 18 months of 20 days with a period of five days at the end. Each day was given two dates that showed its position in both the Tzolk'in and the Haab cycles.

Superstitions

The Maya had many superstitions about dates and would wait until a 'lucky' day to do certain activities. People dreaded the five days at the end of the Haab calendar, which were thought to be very unlucky. During this time, people were scared to work and carried out sacrifices at home to please the gods.

This is part of a codex that gives information about each of the days in the religious Tzolk'in calendar.

Astronomy

In observatories, Mayan astronomers tracked the movements of Venus, the Sun, the Moon and the stars. Over time, they learned to predict eclipses and planned rituals to take place at the same time. The Maya timed wars to begin on days when Venus was in the sky, as this was thought to bring good luck.

This Mayan observatory is in Chichén Itzá, Mexico. Mayan astronomers didn't have any scientific instruments so they tracked planets and stars by lining up their position with the windows in their observatories.

21

Religion

Religion was very important to the Maya. Temples were built in every city, in which kings and priests carried out important rituals to keep the gods happy. These rituals followed the Mayan calendars and happened at the same time every year. At home, commoners had small shrines where they burnt incense and left objects for the gods.

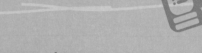

Many gods

The Maya worshipped many gods. Itzamná was the creator of the universe and ruler of the gods and thought to be the inventor of the Mayan language and calendar. His wife, Ixchel, was goddess of the moon. The Maya depended on weather gods such as Chac (the god of rain) and Kinich-Ahau (the sun god) to bring them a good harvest.

This ceramic incense burner in the shape of the rain god, Chac, was probably used in a temple.

One Mayan legend told that the pyramid temple in the city of Uxmal was built in one night by the god Itzamná.

Pyramids and temples

Mayan temples were built on top of tall pyramids so that they would be close to the world of the gods. Only priests, members of the royal family and sacrificial prisoners of war were allowed to climb the steps up to the temple. Crowds of spectators gathered at the base of the pyramid to watch the rituals that took place at the top.

Rituals

Blood was an important part of Mayan rituals. Mayan priests sacrificed prisoners of war and offered their blood to the gods. The Maya believed that kings could speak to their ancestors and the gods through visions caused by bloodletting. In this ritual, kings and members of the royal family cut their tongues or lips and dripped the blood onto a piece of paper.

This stone carving shows Shield Jaguar II, a Mayan king from Yaxchilán, and his wife, Lady Xoc, who is taking part in a bloodletting ritual by pulling a string through her tongue.

23

Make a mosaic mask

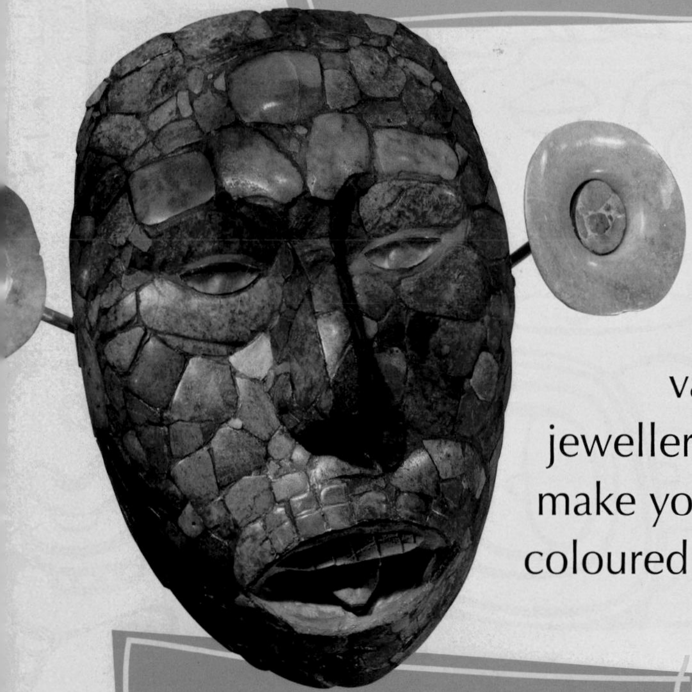

When ordinary Mayans died, they were buried underneath their homes. Members of the royal family were buried in tombs inside pyramids. Their tombs would be filled with valuable items, such as painted pottery, jewellery and jade mosaic masks. You can make your own mosaic mask using card and coloured paper.

1

Cut out the shapes shown here from the different colours of paper and card. Use the drinking glass as a guide to draw the circles.

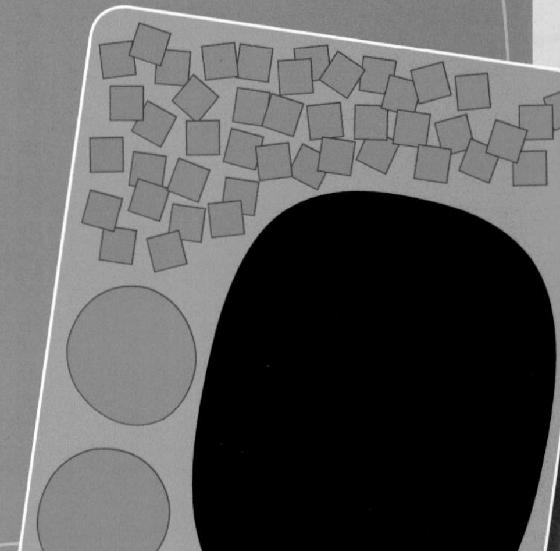

You will need:

an A4 piece of black card

small pieces of white and red paper

an A4 piece of green paper

a drinking glass

a pencil

scissors

a glue stick

approximately 20cm elastic string

2 Use the glue stick to stick your green squares in lines onto the black oval. Repeat until the mask is completely covered. Trim any green squares that hang over the edge of the mask.

3 Stick the eyes, nose, mouth and earrings in place with glue.

4 Carefully cut a hole in the middle of each of the eyes. Then, cut two very small holes just above the earrings. Thread the elastic string through the small holes and knot on each side to fit your head. Your Mayan mask is now complete.

Handy hint
You could use shiny green paper from a magazine instead of plain green paper to make your mask look more like jade!

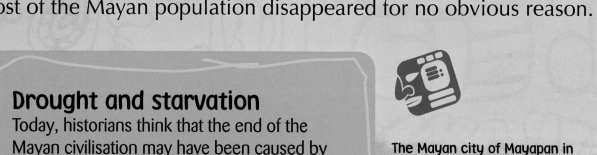

The last Maya

Around CE 900, the Mayan civilisation started to fall apart. Many great cities in the south, such as Tikal, were abandoned, although some cities in Mexico survived until the arrival of the Spanish. Most of the Mayan population disappeared for no obvious reason.

Drought and starvation

Today, historians think that the end of the Mayan civilisation may have been caused by a terrible drought. Without water, the Maya wouldn't have been able to grow crops and so many people died of starvation. Their farming land may have also become less fertile after many years of growing crops. City-states probably fought each other over the remaining food and many people died in battle. However, some Maya moved to more fertile areas in the north and kept the Mayan culture going.

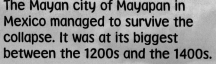

The Mayan city of Mayapan in Mexico managed to survive the collapse. It was at its biggest between the 1200s and the 1400s.

Columbus and conquistadors

After Christopher Columbus's discovery of the continent of North America in 1492, the Spanish were keen to explore Central and South America. They sent over conquistadors (conquerors) to explore and seize land. The Spanish conquistadors first came across the remaining Maya in 1502. By the 1540s, the Spanish had taken most of the Mayan lands and destroyed many artefacts, books and sculptures. They forced the Maya to speak Spanish and become Christians.

The Spanish conquistadors' horses and metal weapons put them at a great advantage against the Maya, who fought on foot with stone-tipped weapons.

Surviving the Spanish

The Spanish made the Maya work on farms or as labourers. Many of the Maya died from working too hard and from new diseases brought from Europe. Some of them escaped into the rainforests and carried on the Mayan culture, living as farmers. Today, there are around 7 million Mayan people living across Central America. Some still speak the Mayan language and practise traditional religious festivals according to the Mayan calendar.

These Mayan girls, wearing traditional woven clothes, live in Guatemala.

Facts and figures

The Maya thought that being cross-eyed was very beautiful. Elite mothers would tie a small ball to a strand of their baby's hair between their eyes. Their babies would stare at the ball so much that they would grow up to be cross-eyed.

As well as the Tzolk'in and Haab calendars, the Maya had a calendar for long periods of time. One cycle of the Long Count calendar was just over 5,125 years.

During the Classic period, as many as 2 million people lived in the Mayan city-states.

The Maya were one of the first civilisations to use a symbol to represent zero. They used dots and bars to represent the other numbers.

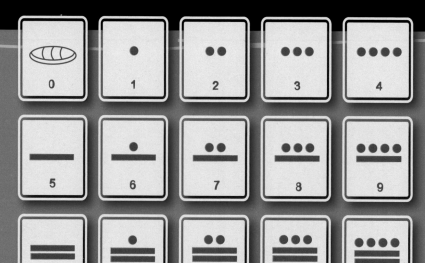

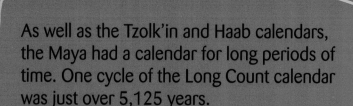

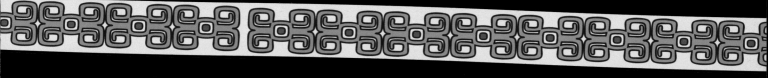

After the Spanish invasion, the Maya stopped using their written language. It wasn't until the 1950s that historians started to learn the meaning of all of the Mayan glyphs again.

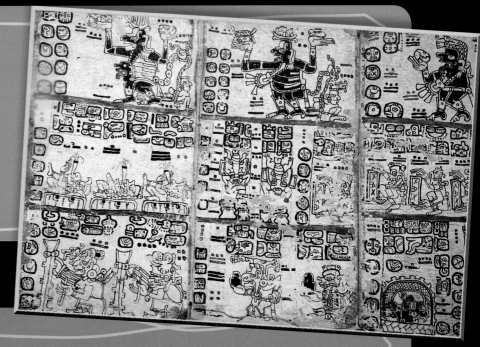

Timeline

9,000 BCE	Ancestors of the Maya arrive in Central America.
50000–2000 BCE	The Maya start farming.
1700 BCE	The Preclassic period begins as the Maya start to settle in villages.
CE 250	The Classic period begins. The Maya build grand cities and develop an advanced civilisation.
900	The Maya start to abandon cities in the south, as the Mayan civilisation starts to fall apart.
900s–1200s	The Toltec rule over central Mexico.
1427	The Aztec Empire takes control over much of Mexico and Central America.
1500s	The Spanish invade and seize Mayan land. Many Maya die from diseases.

Glossary

ancestors People from your family who lived a long time ago

archaeologists People who learn about the past by digging up old objects

artefact An object from the past that reveals information about the people who made it

astronomer Someone who studies the planets, stars and universe

BCE The letters 'BCE' stand for 'before common era'. They refer to dates before CE 1.

bloodletting A ritual that involves making someone bleed on purpose

cacao A tropical tree that has seeds that can be made into chocolate

CE The letters 'CE' stand for 'common era'. They refer to dates from CE 1.

city-state A state made up of a city and the area surrounding it, ruled by one leader

civilisation A well-organised society

climate The weather conditions in an area

codex (codices) Written Mayan records

conquistador One of the Spanish people that travelled to Central and South America in the 16th century and seized the land from native people

drought A long period where there is little or no rain

elite The richest, most-powerful people in a society, second only to the king

fertile Describes land in which you can grow good-quality crops

fictional Made-up or invented

glyph A symbol used to represent a sound or a word in the Mayan written language

hunter-gatherer Someone who lives by hunting and collecting wild foods

jade A precious green stone

mural A painting that is painted on a wall

obsidian A glassy rock formed when volcanic lava cools

resource Things such as rocks and wood that can be found in an area and used by people

ritual A religious ceremony where certain actions are carried out

sacrifice The act of killing an animal or a person because you believe it will make a god happy

scribe Someone who writes and reads documents

shrine A place or building where people offer prayers and gifts to gods

superstition A belief that is based in magic rather than science

territory An area of land that is ruled by a particular leader or group of people

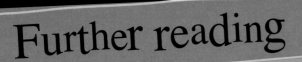

Further reading

Mayan Civilisation (The History Detective Investigates),
Clare Hibbert (Wayland, 2015)

The Maya (Great Civilisations),
Tracey Kelly (Franklin Watts, 2015)

The Maya (Discover Through Craft),
Charlie Samuels (Franklin Watts, 2016)

Websites

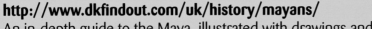

http://www.dkfindout.com/uk/history/mayans/
An in-depth guide to the Maya, illustrated with drawings and photos.

https://maya.nmai.si.edu/maya-sun/maya-math-game
Learn about Mayan numbers and play a simple maths game.

http://www.bbc.co.uk/education/clips/z2pfgk7
Watch a video about a lost Mayan city in Chiapas, Mexico and discover the Mayan people who still live in the area.

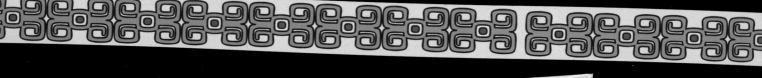

Index